D0382778

Nerdy Birdy

STORY BY
Aaron Reynolds

PICTURES BY
Matt Davies

A NEAL PORTER BOOK
ROARING BROOK PRESS
NEW YORK

For Narsamor, Honorableone, Keirah, Chainrattle, Rendaar,
and all my World of Wormcraft peeps.
—A.R.

For Severn, Larkyn & Keiland. And all your fellow Whovians.
—M.D.

Text copyright © 2015 by Aaron Reynolds
Illustrations copyright © 2015 by Matt Davies
A Neal Porter Book
Published by Roaring Brook Press
Roaring Brook Press is a division of Holtzbrinck Publishing Holdings Limited Partnership
175 Fifth Avenue, New York, New York 10010
The art for this book was created using pen and ink and watercolor on paper.
mackids.com

Library of Congress Cataloging-in-Publication Data

Reynolds, Aaron, 1970–
    Nerdy Birdy / by Aaron Reynolds ; illustrated by Matt Davies. — First
edition.
        pages cm
"A Neal Porter book."
    Summary: "A picture book about a nerdy birdy who just wants to hang out
with the cool birds"— Provided by publisher.
    ISBN 978-1-62672-127-2 (hardback)
    [1. Birds—Fiction. 2. Friendship—Fiction.] I. Davies, Matt (Matthew
Keiland Parry), 1966– illustrator. II. Title.
    PZ7.R33213Ne 2015
    [E]—dc23

                                                    2014044216

Roaring Brook Press books may be purchased for business or promotional use. For information
on bulk purchases please contact Macmillan Corporate and Premium Sales Department
at (800) 221-7945 x5442 or by email at specialmarkets@macmillan.com.

First edition 2015
Book design by Jennifer Browne
Printed in China by Toppan Leefung Printing Ltd., Dongguan City, Guangdong Province

1 3 5 7 9 10 8 6 4 2

This is Nerdy Birdy.

His glasses
are too big.

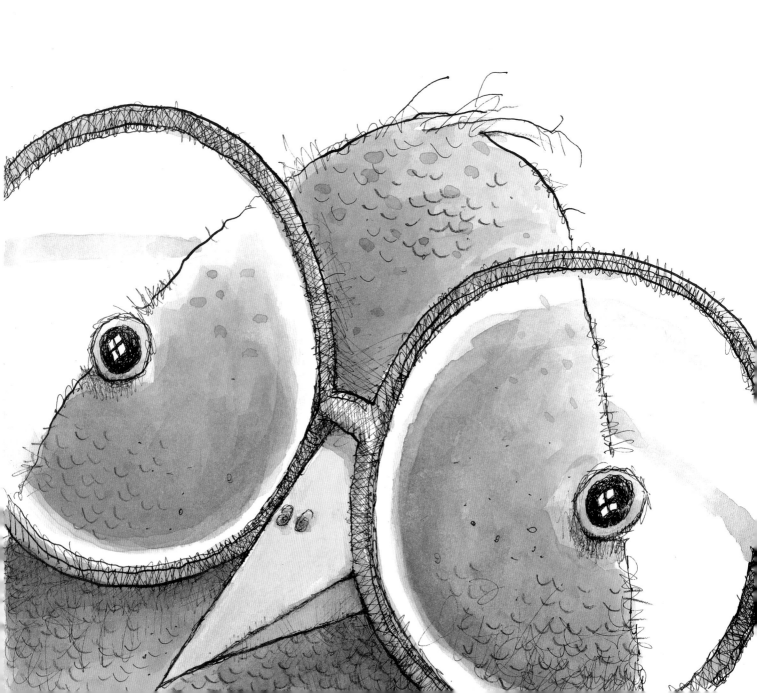

His wings are
too small.

He's allergic
to birdseed.

When all the other
birds are hanging out
together at the
bird feeder,

Nerdy Birdy is scrounging for breadcrumbs.

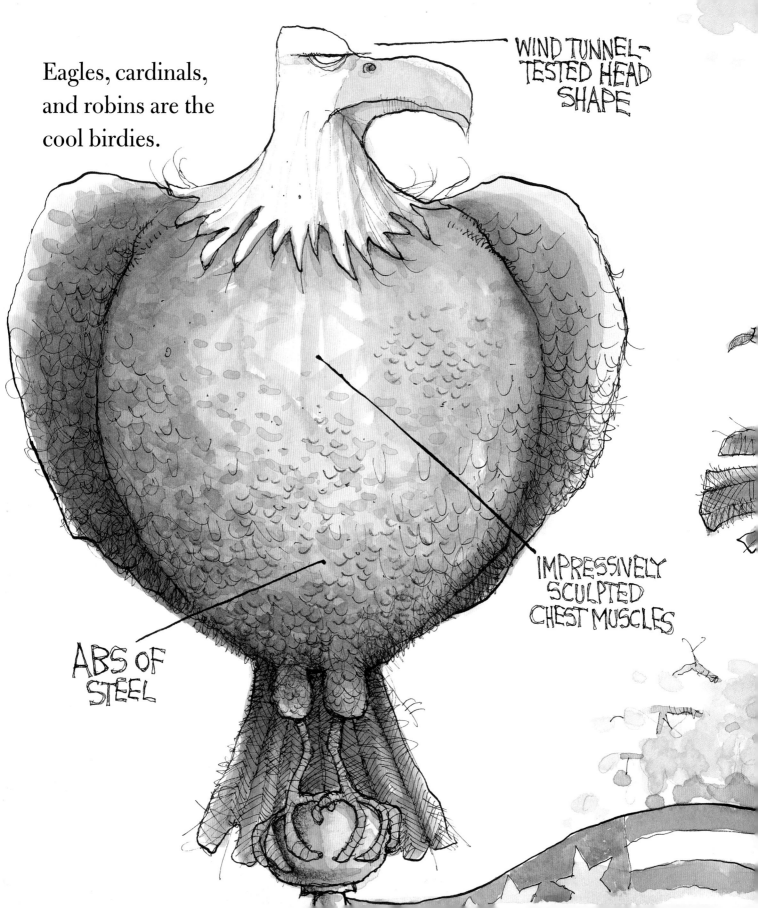

Eagles, cardinals, and robins are the cool birdies.

WIND TUNNEL-
TESTED HEAD
SHAPE

IMPRESSIVELY
SCULPTED
CHEST MUSCLES

ABS OF
STEEL

Three things Eagle is good at:

1. Hunting

2. Fishing

3. Football

Three things Cardinal is good at:

1. Singing like a rock star

2. Posing

3. Attracting fans

Three things Robin is good at:

1. Picking on worms

2. Insulting worms

3. Eating worms

Three things Nerdy Birdy is good at:

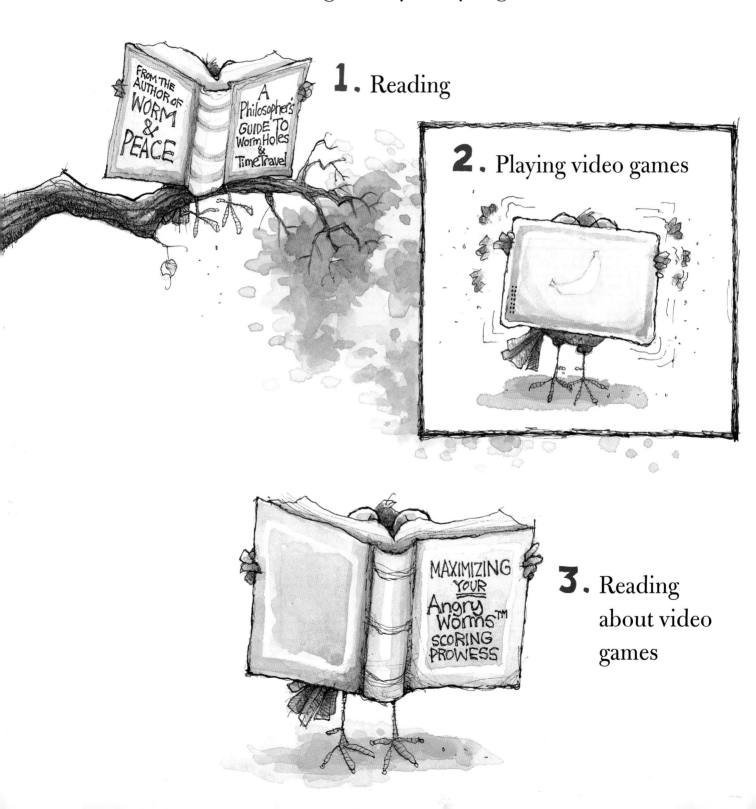

1. Reading

FROM THE
AUTHOR OF
WORM
&
PEACE

A
Philosopher's
GUIDE TO
Worm Holes
&
Time Travel

2. Playing video games

3. Reading
about video
games

MAXIMIZING
YOUR
Angry
Worms™
SCORING
PROWESS

Eagles, cardinals, and robins don't care about reading.

Or video games.

Cardinal flew off
to impress fans.

One day, Eagle
flew off to hunt.

Robin flew off to
terrorize worms.

And Nerdy
Birdy was
alone.

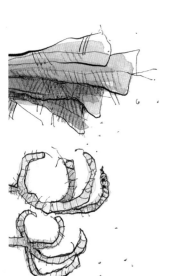

One thing was clear. It was awfully lonely not being a cool birdy.

"US!!"

"AFTER ALL, THERE'S ALWAYS ROOM FOR ANOTHER NERDY BIRDY."

Their glasses were too big.
Their wings were too small.
At least half of them had
birdseed allergies.
They all liked to read.
And most of them liked to play
World of Wormcraft.

They were
exactly like
Nerdy Birdy!

And then he realized something.

There were way more nerdy birdies than cool birdies.

And now they were all his friends.

Eagle didn't have any friends.
Eagle hunted alone.

Cardinal was always
showing off. He had
no friends. Know why?
Because he was always
showing off.

Robin was
too obsessed
with worms to
make friends.

One thing was clear.
It was awful lonely
being a cool birdy.

But then a new bird
moved into the
neighborhood.

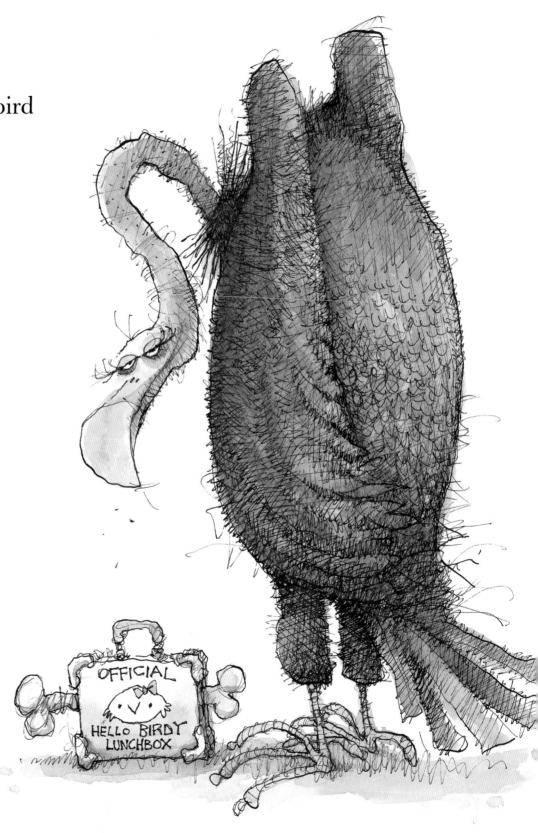

The cool birds were unimpressed.

The cool birdies flew away
and left Vulture alone.

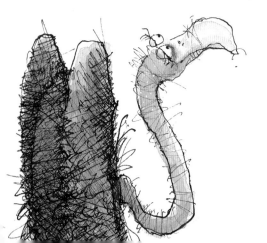

"RIGHT, GUYS?"

"HOLD IT!"

"WHERE ARE HER GLASSES?"

"WHERE IS HER LIGHT SABER?"

"AND HAVE YOU HEARD WHAT SHE EATS?

"BLECCH!!"

"SHE IS MOST DEFINITELY NOT ONE OF US!"

Nerdy Birdy was confused.

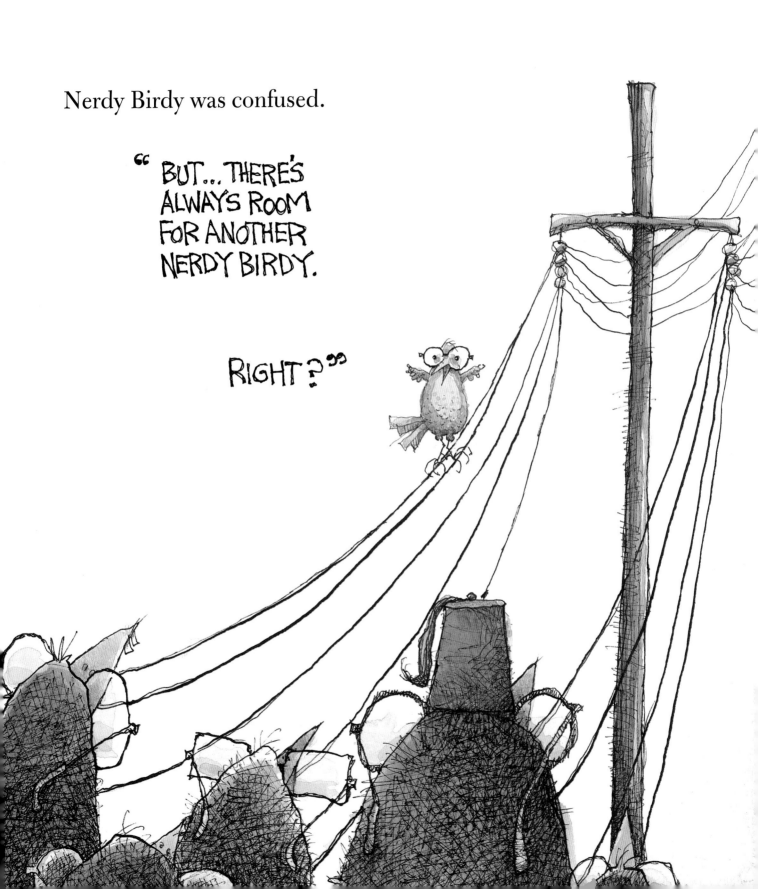

Nerdy Birdy looked at his flock
of friends. The telephone wire
was packed with them.

He looked at the
new bird, sitting
there alone.
And one thing
was clear.

It was awful lonely
being alone.

This is Nerdy Birdy.
His glasses are too big.
His wings are too small.

This is Vulture.
She wears contact lenses.
Her wings are enormous.

Vulture eats dead things.
Nerdy Birdy does not.

Nerdy Birdy likes video
games. Vulture does not.

Nerdy Birdy and
Vulture don't like all
the same things.
But they really like
each other.

If you ever need a friend,
you can hang around with them.

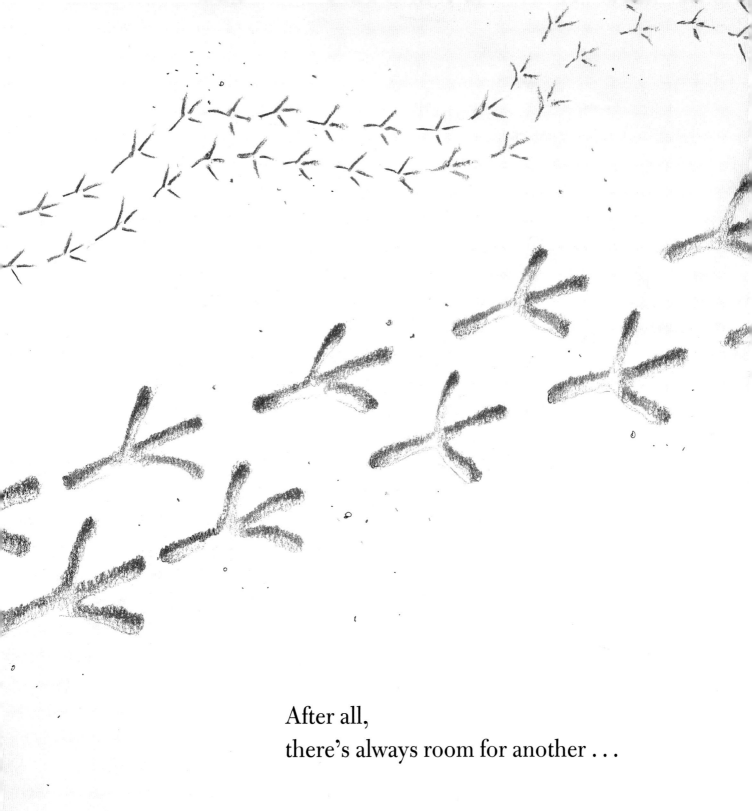

After all,
there's always room for another . . .

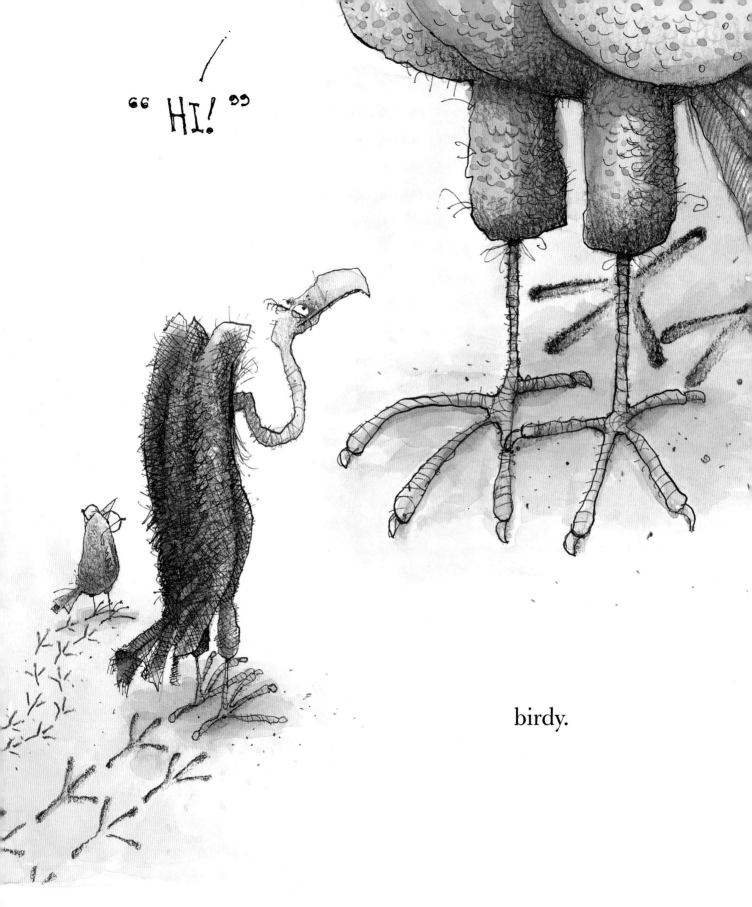

"HI!"

birdy.